This book belongs to

....

Written by Tim Bugbird.
Illustrated by Lara Ede.
Designed by Ellie Fahy.

Molly
the Muffin Fairy

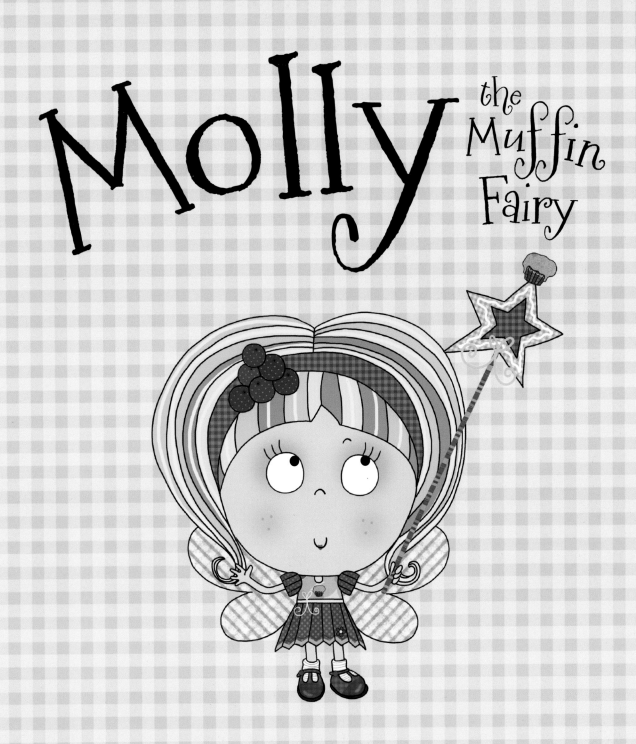

Tim Bugbird · Lara Ede

make
believe
ideas

Molly the Muffin Fairy was famous in Fairyland for making perfect muffins — some small and some quite grand.

Each one was baked 'til spongy,
golden, soft, and sweet.
Her wand put in big blueberries
to make the treats complete!

Blueberries

Blueberries

The blueberries came in boxes, delivered by Mel and Kerri, her two best friends, who drove a truck shaped like a giant berry!

But then one day when baking,
Molly's temper began to fray;

her muffins had no softness —
she was having a bad bake day!

Her baking got **no better,**
and soon **Molly's** fairy home
was full of **rubbery muffins**
with tops as hard as **stone!**

Molly was not happy. The baking was making her MAD!

She fussed and fumed and finally flipped!

What she did was really bad . . .

She grabbed a tray of muffins and threw them to the floor,
then took a muffin in her hand and hurled it out the door!

The muffin hit her trampoline and **bounced** up in the air.

The strangest scene there's **ever** been
followed on from there . . . .

and pinged
and ponged,

It bounced
and bumped

startling a **squirrel**,
who scampered and woke
a **porcupine** down below!

**flying
to** and **fro,**

Up with a **start**, the porcupine **ran**
to find a **safe place** to hide.

But he **poked** the edge of Molly's pool – his **spikes** making **holes** in the side!

Water gushed out from the holes,
flooding the road all around.

Then Mel and Kerri's truck arrived, but **how** would they cross the **wet** ground?

Berry Truck

Blueberries

Blueberries

Molly cried, "It's all a mess!"
Mel said, "Oh, stop whining!
Those muffins of yours could help us —
every cloud has a silver lining!"

"Maybe they could make a **path**. Just try and see."
So **Molly** laid the **muffins** down . . .

and the truck
crossed **easily!**

Then, before the fairies' eyes,
the muffins began to expand.

Soaking up water, they became
the **biggest** in Fairyland!

"The muffins feel soft!" cried Molly.

"Don't eat them, though; they're not clean!

But squashed together, I think they'll make . . ."

"the best-ever trampoline!"

Molly learned that when things look bad, you can always find a way to see things from the **sunny side** and turn around your day!